Finley Flowers

New & Improved

BY JESSICA YOUNG

ILLUSTRATED BY JESSICA SECHERET

PICTURE WINDOW BOOKS
a capstone imprint

Finley Flowers is published by Picture Window Books
A Capstone Imprint
1710 Roe Crest Drive
North Mankato, MN 56003
www.mycapstone.com

Library of Congress Cataloging-in-Publication Data
Young, Jessica (Jessica E.), author.
  New & improved / by Jessica Young; illustrations by
Jessica Secheret.
      pages cm. -- (Finley Flowers)

Summary: For her first assignment in fourth grade, Finley
has to think of an invention that will help the world — but
when her Supersonic Sibling Sublimator appears to work
too well and her annoying older brother vanishes, only to
reappear laughing at the trick he played, Finley comes up
with a new invention she is sure will be a hit.

ISBN: 978-1-4795-6176-6 (hardcover) -- 978-1-4795-5959-6
(paper over board) -- 978-1-4795-9779-6 (paperback)
978-1-4795-6187-2 (eBook PDF) -- 978-1-4795-8590-8
(reflowable epub)

1. Middle-born children--Juvenile fiction. 2. Brothers
and sisters--Juvenile fiction. 3. Inventions--Juvenile
fiction. 4. Elementary schools--Juvenile fiction. [1. Middle-
born children--Fiction. 2. Brothers and sisters--Fiction.
3. Inventions--Fiction. 4. Schools--Fiction.] I. Secheret,
Jessica, illustrator. II. Title. III. Title: New and improved.

  PZ7.Y8657Ne 2015
  813.6--dc23
  [Fic]

                        2014046202

Editor: Alison Deering
Designer: Kristi Carlson

Vector Images: Shutterstock

Printed in the United States of America.
009737F16

For Wesley and Clara, who love
thinking up brand-new things

TABLE OF CONTENTS

Chapter 1
A NICE DEVICE

"I love fourth grade!" Finley Flowers announced to her best friend, Henry Lin, as they walked to their brand-new cubbies in the fourth-grade hall. "This year we're the oldest ones here, the head honchos, the reigning royalty of Glendale Elementary School! Remember what Ms. Bird said? We're role models for all the younger kids."

"That's a lot of pressure," said Henry. "I hope we don't disappoint her."

"We won't," Finley told him as she hung up her jacket. "We're going to dazzle and amaze her. This is going to be our year!"

Finley and Henry were just starting their second week of school. So far it had been Fin-tastic! Their new teacher, Ms. Bird, had caramel-colored eyes that lit up when someone asked a question, and her hands fluttered around when she talked. She said "interesting" a lot, and Finley could tell she really meant it. It seemed like Ms. Bird was interested in everything, including all of Finley's Fin-teresting ideas.

Finley was trying extra hard not to be too hoppity in class — they were still in their getting-to-know-you phase. But sometimes it seemed like Ms. Bird was hoppity, too, flitting up and down the rows of desks as everyone worked.

So far their class had conducted "What-Floats-Your-Boat?" experiments, designing model ships to see which ones were the most buoyant. They'd also built bridges out of pretzels and eaten them at snack time. Finley couldn't wait to see what they'd do next.

When Finley got to her classroom, the first thing she noticed was the giant plastic lightbulb and strands of twinkling lights that hung from the ceiling. At the back of the room, she saw a bulletin board that read "Inventor Center." It was covered with pictures of all kinds of crazy contraptions. A robot dog was scurrying around the classroom, fake-barking and wagging its tail. It stopped next to Finley and Henry, and its eyes lit up with heart symbols. Then it fake-whined and lifted its leg.

"Aaaah — no!" Henry yelped, jumping back. "Do I look like a fire hydrant?"

Finley laughed. "Who brought that to school?"

"Ms. Bird did," Olivia Snotham said from behind her. "Its name is Tesla, after the guy who invented robotics."

"Wow," said Finley. "That's some class pet."

Olivia and Finley had been in the same class since kindergarten. They didn't have much in common, but over the summer they'd been forced to share a cabin at sleep-away camp, and Finley had learned that Olivia wasn't so bad. They were even starting to become friends.

All around the room, students buzzed with excited chatter. Ms. Bird liked the noise level kept to a dull roar, but this was a *real* roar.

That's what happens when you put up twinkling lights and bring a robot dog to school, thought Finley.

Ms. Bird stood beside her desk and rang her magic chime, but it didn't work. Finley could barely hear it over the ruckus. Ms. Bird tried turning off the lights, but that just made things worse.

"CLASS, PLEASE TAKE YOUR SEATS!" a robotic voice boomed. Everyone went silent.

When all the students had settled down, Ms. Bird flicked the lights back on and walked to the front of the room. She cradled Tesla in one hand and held a strange-looking megaphone in the other. "The modern megaphone was invented by Thomas Edison in the late 1800s," she said in her robo-tone, "but I like this newfangled model, complete with voice modulator."

Ms. Bird set the megaphone and Tesla on her desk. "I know you're curious about what we'll be working on," she continued in her regular chirpy voice, "so put on your listening ears."

Finley *was* curious. She glanced at Henry, then put her pencil down and sat at attention.

"Our world is a wonderful place," Ms. Bird said as she drew a giant Earth on the board with a green marker. "But it has some problems, too. Luckily, there's a powerful tool we can use to solve them. Does anyone know what that tool might be?"

Finley didn't know. And from the looks of it, no one else did either.

Ms. Bird perched on her tall stool and folded her hands. She looked confident, like she knew someone was going to come up with the perfect answer at any moment. But judging by her classmates' zombie-like stares, Finley was pretty sure they weren't.

Suddenly, Olivia put up her hand and shook it like her fingers were on fire. "A smartphone!" she shrieked.

"Good guess," said Ms. Bird. "A smartphone *is* a useful tool. However, it's not the tool I have in mind."

Henry raised his hand.

Ms. Bird pointed in his direction. "Henry?"

"The electric drill?"

Ms. Bird smiled. "Electric drills are helpful, too," she said. "But the tool I'm thinking of is something everyone is born with."

Finley pictured a newborn baby holding an electric drill — that was *definitely* not something everyone was born with.

"*Think* about it," Ms. Bird said, tapping the side of her head.

I'm thinking so hard my brain hurts, Finley thought. Then it hit her. "Oh!" she blurted out. "The brain!"

Ms. Bird nodded. "Exactly. Every helpful invention, from the robot dog to the megaphone to the electric drill, started with an idea in a brain like yours. You might think, 'What good can I do? I'm just a kid.' But kids have come up with some amazing inventions."

"Like what?" asked Olivia.

"Like Popsicles," Ms. Bird said, drawing one on the board. "And earmuffs. And trampolines. I bet you'll find a lot more as you research. For our first big class project, I want each of you to design your own invention — a 'nice device' that makes the world a better place."

Ms. Bird finished drawing earmuffs and a trampoline, then added shine lines all around the Earth to show that it had been better-ified.

A kid invented Popsicles? Finley thought. *That does make the world a better place.* She wanted to invent something great, too. Something that would change the world. She raised her hand. "So how do we start?"

Chapter 2

THE NEXT PET ROCK

"Have you ever heard the saying 'necessity is the mother of invention'?" Ms. Bird asked. She strolled to the back of the classroom and paused under the giant lightbulb. "Thinking of a problem or something people need is a great first step to inventing." She pointed to a glossy poster and read, "Information + Inspiration + Imagination + Determination = Innovation."

"What in *tarnation* does that mean?" Henry whispered.

Finley shrugged. She got the "imagination" part, but she wasn't so sure about the rest.

20270768

"That means that research might inspire you to think of an interesting idea," Ms. Bird continued. "And if you stick with your idea and keep trying, you could come up with a great new thing. At the Inventor Center you can find lots of information to get you started."

She gestured to the bookshelves and the tables stacked with magazines. "We'll work on this project all week, and on Friday we'll have an Invention Convention where you'll share your creations with some special guests." She looked at Finley. "I can't wait to see what you come up with."

Me, too, thought Finley.

Olivia waved her hand in the air. "What do we get if we win?" she asked.

"It's not a contest," Ms. Bird explained, "just a chance to learn and meet some expert inventors. You'll get the satisfaction of thinking of a great new idea and sharing it."

"Oh." Olivia slouched in her chair. She looked like her enthusiasm had sprung a leak.

Expert inventors! thought Finley. *I wonder who they could be. Whoever they are, I'm going to come up with something Fin-omenal to show them. It's my first fourth-grade project, and I'm going to make a good impression!*

When Ms. Bird announced it was research time, Finley took a seat at a round table in the Inventor Center with Henry, Olivia, and their other friends, Kate and Lia. She grabbed a magazine and leafed through it. There were designs of flying cars, pictures of musical socks that played notes when you wiggled your toes, and inflatable fortune cookie balloons with messages inside them. There was even a bracelet that could be unraveled and used as dental floss.

"Cool!" said Henry, pointing to a picture in his book. "A Handlebar Mustache! It's a giant mustache that attaches to your bike handlebars. It even has pockets for snacks and drinks."

"What about this Numbrella?" said Lia. "It teaches you math while keeping you dry. It's like a pie chart. When you press different buttons on the handle, the different sections of the pie light up to show fractions."

"Look!" Finley held up her magazine. "It's Gary Dahl — the guy who invented the pet rock. It says here he's sold millions of them. He made more than fifteen million dollars in six months!"

"Selling rocks?" Kate made a face.

"*Pet* rocks," said Finley. "They come with their own special crate and training manual."

"That's ridiculous," said Olivia. "Who wants to have a rock for a pet? They don't fetch or cuddle. They don't even move."

"They can play dead and roll over," Finley pointed out. "And they don't need food or housetraining." She stared at the picture of Gary Dahl. "I want to sell millions of *my* invention. Maybe the expert inventors will tell me how. Or maybe they'll even want to buy my idea. Then I'd be rich and famous! I'd donate half my money to build the school a swimming pool and a skating rink and an awesome new art room with tons of cool supplies. And I'd get Mom and Dad a new car while I'm at it — Mom's always wanted a convertible."

"Sounds good to me," said Henry. "Now you just have to think of something to invent."

Finley stared at her blank paper. Then she flipped it over and stared at the other side. She wished she had some chocolate chips. Chocolate chips always helped her think. At least she could doodle. She took out a pencil and made a circle. She drew a line next to it, then more lines. It looked like a sun. Finley gave it a smile and sunglasses. "Major brainstorm alert!" she announced. "I've got it — glow-in-the-dark sunscreen! I'll bet you've never seen *that* before!"

"Nope," said Olivia. "Probably because people don't need sunscreen when it's dark."

"Glow-in-the-dark *moon*screen might work," Henry suggested.

"Moonscreen?" Olivia rolled her eyes. "You're a space cadet!"

Finley and her friends sat and thought. Henry wrote a column of neatly printed numbers to start an

idea list. He *loved* making lists. Olivia picked little lint balls off her sweater and rolled them into one big lint ball. Finley twirled one of the loose strands of hair that had escaped from her braids. *Maybe if I twirl hard enough*, she thought, *it'll wind up my brain*.

Finley usually had so many new ideas they squeezed out the other thoughts — the ones that helped her remember the capital of Nebraska or where she'd left her sweater. *Why is it easy to think of ideas when you don't need them and hard to think of them when you do?* she wondered.

Henry started whistling "Blue Suede Shoes" as he finished numbering his list. Henry loved Elvis. "Hey," he said, putting his pencil down. "Remember how some of the older kids at Camp Acorn whittled those twig whistles?"

Finley frowned. "Yeah, I remember. I wanted to make one, but they said I was too little to whittle."

"Well, I've got something even better — an edible whistle!" said Henry. "You could blow it, then eat it!"

"*Eat* it?" Olivia made a face.

"Uh-huh," said Henry. "You could wear it around your neck. That way you'd never leave home without a snack."

"Good idea," said Finley. "But what kind of snack could be a whistle?"

"Remember the fruit leather I made in camp cooking class?" Henry asked.

Olivia wrinkled her nose. "Don't remind us."

"I could sculpt whistles out of fruit leather," Henry said. "They could even come in different flavors."

"Yuck," said Olivia.

"You're a genius," said Finley. Ever since the school cook-off, Henry had been coming up with fun, new snacks.

Finley was glad Henry had his idea, but she was still drawing a blank. She flipped through the pages of an *Inventor's Monthly* magazine. Solar-powered water bottle fan, laser toenail clippers, mini-flower-vase barrettes, washable chalkboard doodle-pants. It was a well-known fact that making things was her thing. But could she think of an invention as great as those?

Ms. Bird rang the chime. This time everyone stopped, looked, and listened. "We'll be starting math in five minutes," she said, "so please finish up. I hope you found some interesting information — maybe even some inspiration. But if not, don't worry. Ideas are everywhere. Sometimes you can even get one by playing."

Finley put away her magazine, but she couldn't stop thinking about the Invention Convention. She knew the perfect idea was somewhere in her brain — a tiny seed ready to grow and burst into bloom. She just hoped it would hurry.

Chapter 3

IT'S ALL BEEN DONE BEFORE

When Finley got home, she ran up to her room and opened her toy chest. If Ms. Bird said ideas came from playing, then she was going to play. She took out a purple velvet bag and dug through her old marble collection. She'd forgotten how cool marbles were — how they clinked together and felt so smooth and perfect in her hand. There were big, cloudy glass ones with tiny bubbles, shiny silver steelies that were heavier than the rest, and clear ones that looked like cats' eyes with ribbons of color twisting through the centers.

Finley held an orange-and-blue marble up to the light and admired its swirly stripes. Then she rummaged through the chest and found her old superhero cape. She tied one end of the cape to the back of her desk chair and pulled the other end tight over the seat, tying it to the chair legs.

Finley rolled a marble down the slanted fabric, then flung it back up, launching it off the top of the chair just as her older brother, Zack, opened her bedroom door. The marble flew across the room and pelted him in the stomach.

"Ow!" he said. "Watch it!"

"Sorry," said Finley. "You should have knocked before entering. This is a maximum-security lab."

Zack rolled his eyes. "Mom says it's your turn to set the table. Dinner is in half an hour."

"Wait!" said Finley. "Look what I made! It's a project for school — we have to design our own invention. I call it the Superbly Slanted Slope." She motioned for Zack to move and launched another marble. "So, what do you think?"

Zack raised an eyebrow. "I think it's dangerous. And it's not your invention — it's basically an inclined plane. The ancient Egyptians used them to build the pyramids."

Finley narrowed her eyes. "Are you sure?"

"Sure, I'm sure," Zack said. "Look it up."

"I will," said Finley. "Tell Mom I'll be there in a bit."

"Fine." Zack turned and headed down the hall.

Finley sighed. She didn't have to look it up. Zack was always right about stuff like that. Plus, he'd studied ancient civilizations last year in fifth grade. She remembered his project on mummies. "Great," she mumbled. "Back to the drawing board."

Maybe there's an idea hiding in here, Finley thought as she pulled her junk trunk out of her closet. She threw open the lid and sorted through her heaping collection: a dissected clock, broken building sets, tangles of yarn, pieces of toys, sheets of half-popped Bubble Wrap, rolls of ribbon, duct tape, wrinkled foil, and mountains of paper clips and bottle caps.

Finley grabbed some supplies and set to work. She was trying to build a robot cat out of Popsicle sticks, tinfoil, and rubber bands when her fingers slipped, and its head shot across the room.

Aha! Finley thought. *Inspiration strikes!* She wrapped a rubber band around the ends of two Popsicle sticks and rolled up a long piece of tape, wedging it between the sticks so they made a *V.* Then she crunched some foil into a ball, turned the *V* on its side, set the ball on the end of the top stick, and pressed it down, ready to launch.

Just then, Zack passed by. "How do you like my Stupendous Sphere Slinger?" Finley called.

As Zack poked his head in the doorway, she slid her finger off the end of the stick, and it sprang up, sending the foil ball flying.

"Hey!" Zack yelped, as it hit him between the eyes. "You mean *catapult?* Some Greek guy made them popular more than two thousand years ago."

Finley groaned. As soon as Zack had left, she went to the computer and looked it up. There it was, her very own invention: a catapult. She was getting sick of people stealing her ideas. Even if those people had been dead for centuries.

Finley took out her sketchbook. Maybe she needed to draw up a few plans. She scribbled and labeled. Then she went back to her junk trunk and tinkered and tweaked.

"Zack!" she yelled. "Come look at this!"

"Not now!" he shouted. "I'm playing *Extreme Zombie Picnic*, and I just made it to level ten!"

"Pleeeeeeeease?"

"Oh, all right," Zack said. "But hold your fire." Finley heard him plod down the hall. He peered in, shielding his face with the video-game controller.

"Ta-daaah!" Finley said, holding up a pincer-like contraption. She opened and closed its claws with a scissoring motion and demonstrated picking up a Styrofoam ball. "Introducing the Great Gotcha Grabber!"

Zack shook his head. "Salad tongs. Listen, I don't want to burst your bubble," he said, popping a scrap of Bubble Wrap, "but why don't you just give up? Everything's already been invented."

"Give up?" Finley grabbed her pencil. "Are you kidding? Check out my Fabulous Floaty Flyer!" She pointed to a diagram in her sketchbook.

Zack shrugged. "Looks like a kite to me."

"No problem," Finley told him. "I've got more." She flipped the page. "Spectacular Stick Shooter?"

Zack sighed. "Crossbow. Ancient China."

"Deluxe Dirt Digger?" she said hopefully.

"That would be a garden hoe."

"Load-Lightening Levitator!" Finley said, her voice cracking.

Zack held the video-game controller like a microphone. "Ladies and gentlemen, I give you . . . the pulley," he said in his best TV-announcer voice, "lifting cargo and hoisting sails for thousands of years!"

"Finley Flowers, dinner's ready! Come set the table!" Mom's voice echoed down the hall.

"I'll be right there!" Finley yelled. Then she turned back to Zack. "What about the Monster Mosquito Masher?"

"Fly swatter." Zack fake-yawned. "Been there, done that. Now, are you finished? I'm hungry."

Finley swiped at him with her sketchbook as he turned to leave. "Nope," she told him. "I'm just getting started."

Chapter 4

SUPERSONIC SIBLING SUBLIMATOR

The next day at lunch, Finley was getting ready to eat her dessert first when Henry slid into the seat across from her.

"How's it going?" he asked. "Did you think of an —"

"Don't mention inventions," Finley said, taking a bite of her oatmeal cookie.

Henry frowned. "You didn't come up with anything new and good?"

Finley shook her head glumly. "Not even anything new and *bad*. Nothing's sprouting in my idea garden."

Henry pulled a plastic bag out of his backpack and took out a globby, brownish tube. "If it makes you feel any better, my Fruity Tooter is a complete failure," he said, holding it up. "The cat ate the first one before I had a chance to test it, and this one won't even make a squeak." He blew into the end to demonstrate, and the whistle let out an airy whisper.

"At least you came up with a new idea," said Finley. "All of my inventions were already invented."

"Did you know Ben Franklin invented swim fins when he was only eleven?" Henry said. "If he could do it, so can we." Henry ripped the whistle in half and handed Finley a sticky piece. "Here," he said, cramming the other half into his mouth. "At least it's tasty. I was thinking I might invent something to do with bugs. Or soccer. Or maybe a new kitchen gadget."

Just then a loud burp erupted from one of the third-grade tables.

Olivia set her tray down next to Finley's and glared in that direction. "Someone needs to teach them some manners."

"Maybe you should invent a manners machine," Finley suggested, as she chomped on her fruit leather.

"That's not a bad idea," said Olivia. "The world could use more politeness." Then she poured a cup of apple juice and took a dainty sip with her pinky stuck out.

"I wish *I* could burp like that," Henry said. "I've never been a very good burper."

"That's not something you should aspire to," said Olivia. "We're supposed to be the mature ones and set a good example, remember?"

"I can't help it," said Henry. "It's a skill I've always admired. I wouldn't do it all the time. But if I ever needed to use it, I could — kind of like karate."

"*Needed* to use it?" Olivia rolled her eyes. "When would that happen? If someone challenged you to a burp duel?"

Finley pictured Henry and a belching bandit facing off for a burp battle to the death.

Henry shrugged. "I dunno. Maybe I'd use it at the talent show. I could burp the school song in one breath."

"That might be considered inappropriate," Finley said.

"My manners machine would teach you that there *is* no appropriate time to burp," said Olivia.

Henry took a bite of his sandwich, and his eyes lit up. "Maybe I could invent a burping apparatus — something to help burp-challenged people like me."

"Or maybe not," said Olivia.

Henry ignored her and took out his notebook and pencil. "It'll take some research," he said, sketching out a rough design.

Finley sighed. "Sounds like you guys have big plans. Now *I* just have to come up with an idea."

* * *

After school Finley went straight to her room to experiment. Henry and Olivia had each thought of a problem and then come up with an invention to solve it. *So what's my problem, aside from being invention-less?* she wondered.

Finley was sitting in front of a mountain of mismatched pieces and parts when Zack poked his head in. "Hard at work again?" he said. "I think you need an invention inventor."

"Ha, ha," said Finley. "Very funny. I think *you* need to disappear."

Zack cupped a hand to his ear. "Uh-oh, homework's calling. Good luck, Einstein."

Finley leaped up and shut the door behind him. Zack was such a know-it-all. Especially now that he was in sixth grade. Big brothers were a big problem.

Hey, Finley thought. *Maybe that's it! I could invent something to keep older brothers and sisters from bugging people. Kate's older sister always borrows her skateboard without asking, and Lia's older brother lost her lucky Frisbee. Stuff like that happens all the time. If I could stop it, that would be a great service to humanity.*

Finley spent the rest of the afternoon in her room, drawing, tying, taping, gluing, and building the most useful Fin-vention ever. She was lying on her bed, exhausted, when Zack knocked on the door.

"What was all that racket?" he said. "Where did all of your not-inventions go? And what is that?" He pointed at the chair in the middle of the floor that was rigged up with levers, pulleys, buttons, and a tangle of attachments.

"If you *must* know," said Finley, "I combined my other ideas into an outstandingly original, incredibly ingenious invention."

"Oh, yeah?" Zack said. "What is it?"

"I call it the Supersonic Sibling Sublimator," said Finley.

"That's a mouthful," Zack said, smirking. "What does it do?"

"It sublimates siblings," said Finley. "Older ones, specifically."

"Really?" said Zack. "Sublimates — as in changes them from a solid to a gas?"

"Poof!" Finley snapped her fingers. "Just like that. It's never been done before, and it will make the world a better place."

"Well, what are you waiting for?" Zack picked his way across the mess on the floor. "One sibling at your service. Sign me up — let's test this thing out."

"Are you sure?" Finley asked.

"Absolutely," Zack said. "Let's take it for a spin."

Finley frowned. "Okay, but don't you want to say goodbye to Mom and Dad? I don't know exactly what'll happen once you're sublimated."

Zack shook his head. "You can tell them for me. Besides, can't you just reverse the process and bring me back?"

"Sure," said Finley, trying to sound convincing. "I mean, I *think* I can —"

"I *know* you can," Zack said. "I believe in you." He pointed to the chair. "Is this where I'm supposed to sit?"

Finley nodded.

Zack sat in the chair and looked at her expectantly.

Finley placed a bike helmet with a tinfoil antenna on his head. Suddenly, she was feeling a little queasy. Maybe this wasn't such a great idea after all. Zack was an enormous pain, but did he deserve to be sublimated? "Are you one hundred percent positive about this?" she asked.

Zack adjusted the helmet and gave Finley a cheery thumbs-up. "Ready when you are!"

"Well," Finley said, "good luck." She shook his hand, took a deep breath, and pressed a red button.

Nothing happened.

She tried again. Still nothing.

"Fiddlesticks," she said. "I think it might need a few minor adjustments."

"No worries." Zack grabbed a comic book and propped his feet up on Finley's desk. "Adjust away.

I've got plenty of time. Mom said I can't go anywhere until my homework is done."

Finley crawled around on the floor, tweaking levers and tightening screws. "Almost ready," she said, double-checking her diagrams. "Just one more minute."

Finley finished fine-tuning and did a final inspection. But when she turned around, the chair was empty.

Chapter 5
BRAND-NEW THING

The only trace of Zack was the comic he'd been reading, which now lay on the floor beside the Sublimator. His helmet sat on the chair like an empty shell.

"Great," Finley muttered. "He had one job — to sit in the chair. And somehow he managed to mess it up."

Finley stuck her head into the hallway. "Zack!" she called. "Come back! It's ready!"

There was no reply.

Finley tiptoed down the hall to Zack's room. She could hear the theme song for *Extreme Zombie Picnic*, but when she peeked in, he wasn't there.

She checked the bathroom.

"Zack!" she yelled again.

Finley searched every room in the house, but Zack was nowhere to be found.

Could it be? she thought. *Has he really been sublimated?* Suddenly, she felt all cold and clammy. Her throat tightened, and her stomach got that awful, carsick feeling.

It was almost dinnertime, and Finley was getting desperate. She slunk into the kitchen. "Mom, Dad, have you seen Zack?" she asked, trying to keep her voice sounding breezy.

"Not lately," said Mom.

Finley swallowed hard. "Well, I really need to find him."

"He's around," said Dad. "He was up in his room playing *Extreme Zombie* —"

"I know," Finley said. "Thanks."

Finley ran outside and checked the backyard. "*Za-aaack!*" she shouted. But the only answer was the frantic barking of the yippy dog two doors down and the wail of a distant siren.

At six o'clock, Zack still hadn't turned up. He never missed his favorite show, *Dumb Things People Do to Get on TV*, which would be starting any minute. Finley's stomach sank. It was obvious. Her invention had worked: her sibling had been sublimated.

Finley sprinted to her room. *Pull yourself together,* she thought. *You're the one who sent him away. Surely, you can bring him back.* She re-adjusted every part of the machine. She checked the connections. Then she reversed all the levers and pushed the red button.

Finley counted to ten.

Still no Zack.

She knew what she had to do, and it wasn't going to be easy.

Finley flew downstairs and burst into the kitchen. Her seven-year-old sister, Evie — a big fan of all things spooky — was reading her *Haunted Homes & Gardens* magazine, and Mom and Dad were busy cooking. They looked so normal. So happy. So unsuspecting. Not like people whose only son had just been zapped into nothingness by their very own daughter.

Savor these last blissful moments of ignorance, Finley thought. Then she gathered up her courage. "Hey, Mom," she said. "Hey, Dad."

Mom stirred a pot on the stove. "Hi, honey. What's up?" she said without turning around.

"Um . . . kind of a lot." Finley cleared her throat. "It's about Zack."

"What did he do now?" Dad asked as he rummaged around in the fridge.

"Well, actually nothing," Finley replied. "He was helping me with a project for school, and —"

"That's great," Mom said. "I've noticed you two have been making a real effort to get along lately."

Finley sighed. There was no easy way to break the news. She'd have to just come right out and say it. She took a big breath. "Zack's disappeared, and it's all my fault. I zapped him with my Supersonic Sibling Sublimator, and he's gone forever, and I'm so, so sorry!" Tears filled her eyes, and she ran out of the kitchen.

As she turned the corner into the living room, Finley tripped over something big and plowed into the coffee table, banging her knee. She looked back to see Zack rolling on the rug, laughing hysterically.

"*Ba-ha-haa-haaaaa!* I can't believe you fell for that!" he said between gasps. "I've been following you around this whole time!"

Finley froze. Her cheeks flamed. Suddenly, she
was sorry he hadn't been sublimated. "Oooh!" she
said, pointing a finger at him. "Just wait till I get that
thing working!" Then she gave him a final glare and
stomped upstairs.

* * *

Finley was lying on her bed, plotting revenge, when Zack pushed her door open a crack and peeked in.

"Out!" she yelled. "Out! Out! Out!"

"Aw, lighten up," Zack said. "Mom and Dad said I had to come apologize. I was just joking. You need to learn how to laugh things off."

"Easy for you to say," Finley said, pouting. "You aren't the one who thought you permanently disappeared someone. And you don't have a big invention project due in three days and nothing to show for it."

Zack shrugged. "If you want, I can pretend to disappear again. Then you can say your invention worked. And *I* could miss school."

Finley shook her head. "But it *doesn't* work. That wouldn't be helping anyone. And that's the whole point of the project."

"It'd be helping *me*," said Zack. "I have a math test Friday."

"No thanks," said Finley. "I need a brand-new thing. I have to come up with another invention that actually works."

"Suit yourself," said Zack, turning to go. "But remember my offer. I'd much rather be sublimated than take that test."

Finley sighed. She'd thought the Invention Convention was going to be fun, but it was turning out to be a real fun-fail. Coming up with a million-dollar idea was seriously stressful. Zack was right about one thing — she could use a good laugh.

Wait a minute! Finley thought, sitting up straight in bed. *That's it!*

She ran to the computer and did a quick search. Then she grabbed her sketchbook.

Chapter 6

JOY TO THE WORLD

The next morning, Ms. Bird gave the class extra free time before recess. Finley, Henry, and Olivia raced over to the Inventor Center.

"The week's half over, but I finally have an idea," said Finley. "And this time it's going to work!"

"I knew you'd think of something," Henry said. "Your idea-sprouting Flower Power never fails. So, what is it?"

"I'm going to invent a laugh machine to bring joy to the world!" Finley announced.

"*Joooy tooo the wooorld!*" Henry sang. "Sounds like a plan."

"How does it work?" Olivia asked.

"I haven't exactly figured that part out yet," Finley admitted. "But I did some research, just like Ms. Bird said, and I discovered that laughing is healthy — studies show it can even help you live longer."

"Wow!" said Henry. "Laughing is serious."

"I guess laughter really is the best medicine," said Olivia.

Finley nodded. "My machine is going to help people live longer and have fun doing it," she said. "All I have to do is figure out how to make them laugh."

"That's easy," Henry said. "Jokes!"

"Good idea! You're the joke expert," said Finley. "Want to help me come up with some?"

"Okey-jokey," Henry said. "We'll make a list — knock-knocks, riddles — anything *pun*-ny!"

"Great!" Finley said. "We can write down all your best ones, then I'll put them together into a joke book and attach it to my invention."

"So what's the rest of your invention?" Olivia asked.

"I don't know yet," said Finley. "I'm making it up as I go. So far it's just a cardboard box with the words *LaughCrafter* printed on the side."

"Jokes are a great start for a laugh machine," Henry said. "Guess what? I found out that *burps* are good for you, too."

Olivia narrowed her eyes at him. "No, they're not."

Henry nodded. "It's true. When you swallow food and drink, air goes down with them. If the air gets trapped in there, it can make you feel sick. So you've got to let it out — in the form of a burp!"

"What if you don't *want* to burp?" Olivia asked.

Henry shrugged. "I guess you could hold it. But it'd come out in the end."

"Ha, ha!" Finley laughed. "The *end*!"

"A burp is but a bit of wind that cometh from the heart," said Henry. "But when it takes the downward route, it cometh as a —"

"Gross!" Olivia made a face.

"Makes burping sound a lot more appealing, doesn't it?" Henry grinned, dimples creasing his cheeks.

"You're not really making some kind of burp device for the Invention Convention, are you?" Olivia wrinkled her nose.

"Why not?" said Henry. "It will improve life for people who have trouble burping. It's almost finished. I call it . . . The Burpolator."

"What do you think Ms. Bird will think of The Burpolator?" Olivia asked.

"Once she hears my presentation, she'll probably want to try it out," said Henry.

Finley pictured Ms. Bird burping. "Ms. Burp," she said. "Now *that's* funny. But seriously, I need some jokes."

"Okay," said Henry. "What did the digital clock say to the grandfather clock?"

"I dunno," said Finley.

"Look, grandpa — no hands!" Henry held his hands up.

"Ha!" said Finley. "Good one!"

"Don't you worry," Henry told her. "We'll have those experts rolling on the floor."

Finley smiled to herself. This was going to be her Fin-niest creation yet!

Chapter 7
SENSE-OF-HUMOR TEST

After school, Finley made a book out of notebook paper and bound it with swirly-patterned duct tape. She copied down the list of jokes Henry had given her and wrote "READ ME" on the cover.

"Time to test out LaughCrafter attachment number one," she said, flipping through the pages.

Finley ran downstairs to her parents' home office. Mom was sitting at the computer, writing. "Hey, Mom," Finley said, "why do spiders use computers?"

"Hmmm?" Mom mumbled without looking up.

Finley didn't wait for an answer. "To build their websites! Get it?"

"Mm-hmm . . ." Mom's fingers kept tapping out a rhythm on the keyboard.

"Never mind," Finley said under her breath. Mom probably wasn't the best test subject anyway. She always thought things were funny that weren't funny and didn't laugh at things that were.

Finley headed to the kitchen next. She found Dad making his famous Scottish black lasagna, which was known for its overcooked, extra-crunchy top. "Knock, knock!" she said.

"Come on in," Dad said, spooning sauce into a casserole dish.

"No, *knock, knock*."

Dad glanced up, a limp lasagna noodle in hand.

"Who's there?" Finley hinted.

"Oh!" said Dad. "Who's there?"

"Hatch."

"Hatch who?" Dad said.

"Bless you!" Finley grinned.

"Nice one," said Dad.

Finley frowned. "I thought it was funny."

"It *is* funny," Dad said as he sprinkled cheese on the noodles.

"Then why aren't you laughing?"

Dad looked at Finley. "I don't know," he said. "I guess something really has to tickle my funny bone to make me laugh out loud. That was a good one, though. Very clever."

"Thanks," Finley muttered. Then she left him to his lasagna.

In the living room, Evie had spread out her dolls on the floor and was painting Cute Little Cupcake's hair with green nail polish.

"What are you doing?" Finley asked.

"Spookifying my dolls," Evie said. "They're much more interesting that way. What are you doing?"

"Working on my invention project for school," said Finley. "Hey, speaking of spooky, where do little ghosts sit on car trips?"

"Beats me," Evie said.

"Boo-ster seats!"

"Har, har," said Evie, carefully applying another coat of green goo to Cupcake's curls.

Finley flipped to a new page in her joke book. "Where do spirits shop?"

"The ghostery store?" Evie guessed.

"Um . . . yeah," said Finley. "Funny, right?"

"Yeah," Evie echoed. "Funny."

"But this is *really* funny — why didn't the ghost pass the test?"

Evie shrugged.

"Because he didn't believe in himself," said Finley. "Get it?"

Evie shook her head. "Not really," she said. "Hey, why all the jokes? What is this?"

"It's a sense-of-humor test," said Finley, "and you just failed it."

Finley turned and stomped back up to her room. She hated to admit it, but *she* was the one who'd failed. *People laugh all the time*, she thought. *So why is it so hard to make them?*

Chapter 8
JUST FOR LAUGHS

Finley grabbed her sketchbook off her bed. *I need better jokes*, she thought. *Some guaranteed giggle-getters.*

When Finley went back downstairs, Evie was camped out in front of the TV. *The Mew Crew* was one of Evie's favorite shows, although Finley couldn't see why. It was about a bunch of talking cats that ran around their neighborhood helping pets in trouble. It wasn't even funny, but sometimes Evie laughed so hard Finley thought she might hyperventilate.

As Finley watched, one of the cats on the show knocked over a glass of milk, and five kittens came pitter-pattering to drink it. Evie burst into hysterical giggles.

"What's so hilarious about that?" Finley asked.

Evie shrugged. "I dunno. It just *is*. Listen — everyone else is laughing, too."

Finley listened. Sure enough, a wave of laughter swept over the invisible TV audience.

"Those aren't real people," Zack said as he passed by with a tray of snacks. "They're canned laughs."

"Canned laughs?" Evie scrunched up her nose.

"Also known as a laugh track," Zack said. "It's a recording of people laughing. They play it after the jokes to make you think they're funny."

"Huh," Evie said. "It works."

"But that's cheating," said Finley. "The laughs are fake."

"It doesn't matter." Zack nodded at Evie. "Look at her."

As if to prove his point, Evie erupted in another giggle fit.

"Laughs are contagious," Zack explained. "Hearing them makes people laugh. TV shows are just using that to their advantage." He turned and headed upstairs.

Huh, Finley thought. *Maybe I don't need better jokes after all. Maybe I need canned laughs.*

She ran to her room and got her mini voice recorder. Then she plopped down on the floor and scooted in close to Evie. As soon as Evie started giggling, Finley pressed record. After a couple of minutes, she had plenty of homemade canned laughs. *It's only Evie*, she thought. *But maybe I can sample some more.*

Finley tiptoed upstairs and down the hall to Zack's room. She dropped to her hands and knees and peered through the door. Zack's friend Sam had come over to play video games, and they were in the middle of an intergalactic space battle. Finley crept up behind Zack's chair.

Suddenly, he spun around to face her. "What are you doing in my room?" he demanded.

"Nothing," Finley said, hiding the recorder behind her back.

"Nothing?" Zack put out his hand and made a give-it-here motion with his fingers.

Finley sighed. Busted. She passed him the recorder. "I'm just trying to catch some laughs."

Zack raised an eyebrow. "You're recording them?"

Finley nodded. "It's my own laugh library. I'm going to use it as a canned-laughs attachment for my invention. If you let me record yours, you guys will be famous, and you'll be helping millions of people live longer, happier lives. Plus, you owe me one after your disappearing act."

Zach grinned. "We'll give it our best, then."

Zack and Sam exchanged looks, then exploded into laughter.

"BAAA-HA-HAAA! HEEE-HEEEEEE-HOOO!"

"A-HAHAHAHAHAHAHAAAA!"

"TEEEE-HE-HEEEE!"

"HOOOO-EEEEE!"

"Thanks," Finley said. "That'll do."

"*N-YUK, N-YUK, N-YUK!*"

"*HEEE-HEEEE! HA-HA-HA-HAAAA!*"

Finley covered her ears. "ALL RIGHT!" she yelled. "THAT'S GOOD, THANKS!"

"No problem," Zack said, taking a bow. "We're here to help."

* * *

It took her a while, but Finley managed to capture a good collection of laughs. Dad had two types: a cheerful, clucking chuckle and a knee-slapping wheeze that left him gasping for air. Evie did her standard giggle-and-shriek. And Mom's high-pitched cackle erupted suddenly like a volcano.

The more Finley thought about it, the more she realized that laughs were mysterious. Somehow, they popped up out of nowhere and took over.

When Henry really got going, he made a noise like a barking seal. Once Kate had laughed so hard she'd peed her pants. And another time in the lunchroom, Henry had told a joke, and Finley had spewed chocolate milk out her nose. That part hadn't been so funny — especially to the lunchroom supervisor.

Whatever laughs were, Finley hoped that once the experts heard them, they wouldn't be able to resist joining in. Clearly, everyone had different funny bones, so the more LaughCrafter attachments, the better. Right now all she had was a cardboard box holding a joke book and canned laughs. Finley planned to keep her eyes peeled for anything else remotely hilarious. She was going funny hunting.

Chapter 9
FUNNY FACE

The next morning, Finley went to school armed with her sketchbook and a pencil. She had one more day till the Invention Convention. It was time to get serious.

All through math, Finley was alert and ready for when something funny came her way. Unfortunately, nothing did — just plain old decimals and word problems about people buying fruit and taking boring car trips to visit their grandma in Indiana. Silent reading was the same. It didn't help that her book was on the Boston Tea Party, which turned out to be way less fun than it sounded.

At snack time, Finley was washing her hands in the classroom sink, daydreaming about what color convertible she'd buy after selling her invention, when she caught a glimpse of her crooked reflection in the faucet. Her head was bulging, her eyes were buggy, and her nose looked like a huge hot dog with freckles.

Now, that's funny, Finley thought. She ran to get Henry.

"Check it out," she said, pointing to the faucet. "It messes up your face."

Henry leaned in for a closer look. "Cool!" he said. "It's like a funhouse mirror."

"Maybe I can add it to the LaughCrafter," said Finley. "A funny-face attachment would be perfect!"

Finley and Henry tried making different faces. They crossed their eyes and did fishy lips. They stuck out their tongues and puffed up their cheeks. They pretended to be aliens. "Take me to your leader," they said, waving their arms around. They were so busy cracking up, they didn't notice Olivia watching.

"What are you guys doing?" she asked.

Finley had her fingers hooked in the sides of her mouth. She turned to face Olivia. "Wesearch!" she said. "Twy it! Iff fum!"

"Fum?" Olivia echoed.

Finley took her fingers out of her mouth. *"Fun.* We're researching funny things for my invention," she explained, pointing to the reflection. "Look — your face is all warped."

"You're warped," Olivia said, peering into the faucet. "Yikes! That's going to give me bad dreams."

"I'm going to add it to the LaughCrafter," Finley said as they all headed back to the snack table.

"How are you going to attach it?" Olivia asked. "You can't bring the whole sink."

Finley frowned. "True . . ."

"You need something more portable," Henry said, opening his applesauce. "What else is curved and shiny?"

"Spoons!" Finley said, pointing to the one in Henry's hand.

Olivia shook her head. "Not big enough."

"Hubcaps!" said Henry.

Olivia rolled her eyes. "*Too* big. Plus, where is she going to get a hubcap by tomorrow?"

Henry shrugged. "She could borrow one off a car."

"Not worth the jail time," Olivia said, nibbling her granola bar. "What about mixing bowls?"

"Our mixing bowls are glass," said Finley.

"You can use one of our metal ones," Henry offered. "Mom and Dad never do. I can drop it off on the way to soccer."

"Thanks," said Finley. "Now I've got three attachments: a joke book, canned laughs, and a funny-face-maker."

"Well, I've already finished my invention," Olivia said, pulling out her sparkly purple notebook. "Check it out — here's a sketch."

Finley stared at the picture. It looked like Evie's hairdressing doll — the one that was just a big head so you could style its hair. Evie had turned hers into Medusa by coloring the hair with black marker and gluing plastic snakes on it, but the one in Olivia's sketch had a hair bow and perfect blond ringlets.

"Meet Miss Manners," said Olivia. "She can help you remember which fork to use first, teach you to say 'excuse me' in five languages, and give directions for writing a proper thank-you letter."

"Wow," said Henry. "How does she work?"

"First, you decide which manners question you need help with," Olivia explained. "Then you press the button, and Miss Manners recites the answer. Well, she doesn't really — she's actually an old Salon Style Doll. I made a recording of my voice answering each question. Here — you pick a question, and I'll pretend to be Miss Manners."

"Hmm . . ." said Henry. "I've always wondered how to tie a bowtie, or what to say if I meet the Queen. Can Miss Manners tell me that?"

Olivia sighed. "No. You have to pick one of the questions printed on the display." She pointed to the diagram in her notebook.

"What about this one?" said Finley. "Where should you put your napkin when you're eating?" She pressed the button next to the question.

"Miss Manners says, 'In your lap,'" Olivia recited in a syrupy-sweet voice.

"I usually stuff mine in the front of my shirt," said Henry. "Like a bib."

Olivia rolled her eyes. "Why am I not surprised?"

"There's just one problem with Miss Manners," said Henry. "People all over the world do things differently. In some cultures, it's even polite to burp. It tells people you enjoyed your meal. I can't wait to show you The Burpolator. It's going to help a lot of burp-less people."

"Miss Manners still says *no burping*," said Olivia. Then she drew a "NO BURPING" sign beside Miss Manners's head in her notebook.

"The cool thing about laughing is that everyone does it," said Finley. "All around the world, babies start laughing when they're only a few months old. So my invention can be used anywhere."

"Everyone can learn to burp, too," said Henry. "It's completely natural."

"A lot of things are completely natural," said Olivia. "But that doesn't mean they're polite."

"Hopefully the visitors will like all of our inventions," said Finley. "Maybe they'll even want to buy them. We'll make the world a better place and make millions at the same time!"

"Bring on the experts!" Olivia announced. "I'm ready for tomorrow!"

Finley was not so ready. She liked the idea of the LaughCrafter, but it didn't seem finished just yet. *Jokes and canned laughs and funny faces aren't enough*, she thought. *I need something more. Something stronger. But what?*

Chapter 10
TICKLE TIME

After school, Finley was sitting at the kitchen table, staring at her reflection in the mixing bowl Henry had brought her. Mom walked by with a basket of laundry and stopped to sample a spoonful of soup from the pot on the stove. "Why so glum, chum?" she asked. "Is something wrong?"

Finley sighed. "The Invention Convention is tomorrow, and I'm trying to come up with things that tickle people's funny bones." Her eyes widened. "*Tickles!* Why didn't I think of that before?"

"Your dad's feet are so ticklish, he can't go barefoot on the lawn," Mom said.

Wow, Finley thought. Come to think of it, she'd never seen him walk on the grass without shoes. And Henry was super ticklish, too.

"Thanks, Mom!" Finley ran to her room, taking the stairs two at a time. *This is great!* she thought. *Tickles are the ticket!*

Finley pulled her craft box out from under her bed and dug through a bag of multi-colored feathers. She picked out an extra-fuzzy one, tugged off her sock, and tested it on her toes. It felt weird — kind of annoying, but not tickly.

"What are you doing?" Evie asked, peeking in the half-open door.

"Trying to make a toe-tickler attachment for my laugh machine," Finley told her. "But I don't think it works."

"It's hard to tickle yourself," Evie said. "Here, let me help."

Finley stuck out her foot, and Evie swept the feather back and forth along Finley's toes. Nothing happened.

"Huh," Evie said. "Maybe you're not ticklish." She tried it on herself and burst into giggles. "But I am!"

"So is Dad," said Finley. "You must have gotten it from him." She shook the rest of the feathers out of the bag and watched them drift down like rainbow snow. "At least it works on someone."

It would be best if the special guests didn't have to tickle themselves, Finley decided. It seemed like an important part of tickling was having it done to you by someone else. But she couldn't ask them to tickle each other. She needed a tickling tool.

Finley searched the basement and dug up Zack's old hamster's cage. She pulled off the lid and took out the hamster wheel, then snuck back upstairs. It had been three years since Hank the hamster had escaped into the weedy woods that bordered the backyard. Surely Zack wouldn't mind her putting the toy to good use.

Finley taped feathers all around the outside of the wheel so they stood up like a fluffy forest of tickly trees. Then she duct taped the wheel to the top of the LaughCrafter and called Evie back to her room.

"All right," Finley said, "let's see if it works."

Evie spun the wheel and held her foot so the feathers brushed the bottom. She giggled and wiggled her toes. "It works!" she shrieked. "You try!" Then she spun the wheel again.

Finley held her foot up and let the feathers graze it. *Funny,* she thought, *but not laugh-out-loud funny.* "I dunno," she said. "I think I need a back-up plan."

"You've already got the jokes, the canned laughs, the funny-face-maker, *and* the toe-tickler," Evie reminded her.

Finley smiled. "I guess you're right. I've got Plans A, B, C, and D. The LaughCrafter is sure to be E for 'excellent!'"

Chapter 11
TOTALLY TONGUE-TIED

On Friday morning, Ms. Bird stood outside the classroom door, greeting the students as they arrived. "Welcome to the Invention Convention!" she said. "Get ready to show us your ingenious ideas!"

Finley, Henry, and Olivia lugged their stuff to their desks and started assembling their inventions. Finley couldn't wait to demonstrate the LaughCrafter. She smiled to herself as she unpacked the attachments and instruction sheets. Then she secured the funny-face-maker to the side of the box with duct tape.

Fame and fortune, here I come! she thought as she gave the toe-tickler a quick spin.

All over the room, students were setting up their nice devices. Every desk displayed a different doodad, gizmo, or thingamajig. *The world is about to be better-ified*, Finley thought, *starting right here at Glendale Elementary.*

Henry took The Burpolator out of its box and uncoiled the plastic tubes that hung from its lid. "Get ready for some beautiful belches!" he announced.

"Whoa," Finley said, "that's a cool contraption!"

"Interesting," said Olivia.

Henry beamed. "Just wait till you see it in action."

Olivia draped a purple tablecloth over her desk and arranged Miss Manners and her accessories on lace doilies. She added a model place setting and a bouquet of fake flowers. Then she put on her white gloves and a ribbon-y, wide-brimmed hat. When she was done, it looked like she and Miss Manners were having tea for two.

Just as everyone finished setting up, the visitors arrived. "Attention please!" Ms. Bird called. "I'd like to introduce our special guests. This is Mr. Wingnutt." She gestured to a balding man with a gray mustache and beard. "He's an aerospace engineer. He's designed many things, most recently some special panels for the International Space Station."

Mr. Wingnutt nodded.

"Gallopin' galaxies," Henry said under his breath.

"Next to him is Dr. Clunk," Ms. Bird continued, "President of Clunk Industries. She invented the collapsible toilet plunger." Dr. Clunk clutched her clipboard and surveyed the class like she was observing a new species of animal. She looked seriously serious. Finley wondered if she had a funny bone in her body.

"Sheesh," Henry muttered. "She should have invented a better name."

"Finally," Ms. Bird went on, "this is Mr. Quackenbottom, inventor of the world's first coffee filters made from recycled elephant dung."

"Really?" Finley whispered to Henry, her eyes wide.

"Gross!" Henry made a face.

Mr. Quackenbottom gave a nervous smile and a wave.

"These experts are all very excited to be here at our fourth-grade Invention Convention!" Ms. Bird said, clasping her hands together. "They can't wait to see your inventions in action!"

Yikes, thought Finley. *If that's what excited looks like, I'd hate to see calm.*

"Our visitors will be coming around to test out your inventions one by one," Ms. Bird explained, "so please be ready to demonstrate your device when it's your turn. After the Invention Convention is over, you'll get written feedback about your creations. Remember, we're all here to learn — so just have fun with it."

"I sure hope the LaughCrafter works," Finley whispered to Henry. "The special guests look like they could use a laugh."

Mr. Wingnutt, Dr. Clunk, and Mr. Quackenbottom walked to the end of the row, clipboards and pens poised.

First up was a boy named Arpin. He'd invented flavored snow paint.

"It's just drink mix and water in a spray bottle," Olivia whispered to Finley and Henry.

"I think it's cool," said Henry. "Now you can eat the yellow snow."

Next in line was Lia with her Hammock Hairband. "I wove it out of really thin yarn," she explained. "It unwinds and transforms into a hammock in case you're stuck somewhere and need an emergency nap."

"Wow," said Finley. "My dad could use one of those."

"Hey, there's Will," said Henry, pointing to the far side of the room. "I really want to check out his Reusable Space Candy. He told me about it at soccer practice. It's part gum, part candy, and it lasts a super-long time so you can use it again and again. Wanna come?"

"You two go ahead," said Olivia. "Gum's not my thing. My mom says it's impolite and that chewing it makes you look like a cow."

"Moo!" said Finley.

"Okay," Henry said. "We'll be right back. Just give a wave if it's our turn."

Finley followed Henry over to Will's desk.

"Mind if we sample some gum?" Henry asked.

"Sure, go ahead," said Will. "You'll be the first to try it — besides me, of course. But I only took a tiny taste." He held up a sticky, grayish hunk. "Ready to go where no kids have gone before?"

"Cool!" said Henry. "It looks like an asteroid." He took the glob and popped it into his mouth.

"Thanks," said Finley, biting off a chunk of hers. She started to chew, but as soon as the gum hit her tongue, it hardened up. It was tough, gritty, and chalky, with a hint of fake strawberry flavor. She tried to blow a bubble, but it stuck to the back of her teeth.

It looked like Henry was having the same problem. His brow furrowed as he worked his jaw from side to side. "Iff tuck," he said to Will.

"What?" Will leaned in closer.

"*Iff tuck.*" Henry pointed to his mouth. "*Elp.*"

Finley looked at the remaining candy in her hand. She tried to shake it off into the trash, but it clung to her fingers like crazy glue.

"Wha di doo pook un dere?" she asked Will.

"Huh?" said Will.

"Un *dere*," Finley said, pointing to the "Reusable Space Candy" sign on his desk.

"Oh!" Will said. "What did I put in there?"

Finley nodded.

"I can't tell you," Will said. "It's my secret formula."

Henry's eyes were bugging out, and the crinkles in his forehead had deepened into creases of concern.

"It's nothing bad," Will assured them. "It's all edible. At least I *think* it is."

Finley poked and prodded the candy with her tongue, but it wouldn't budge. As she watched the experts asking questions and making notes, her stomach got a jittery-skittery feeling. Soon it would be her turn, and she was totally tongue-tied.

Olivia was up next. Finley and Henry looked on as she held out her poofy purple dress and curtsied politely, then showed off her model place setting, complete with salad fork, bread-and-butter plate, teacup and saucer, and a big red sign that said "NO BURPING."

Mr. Wingnutt, Dr. Clunk, and Mr. Quackenbottom watched as Olivia demonstrated her invention. They pushed buttons and listened as Miss Manners gave them advice, which they hastily jotted down like they were taking a test. Push, scribble. Push, scribble. Finally, they shook Olivia's white-gloved hand, practicing her firm-and-friendly handshake technique. Then they moved on to Henry's desk.

Olivia glanced over at Finley and Henry and waved her hands like she was drowning. Henry waved back and gave her the hold-on-just-one-minute signal.

Finley and Henry pulled and pried, but they couldn't dislodge the Reusable Space Candy. As she tugged and twisted the alien gum, Finley spotted Principal Small talking to Ms. Bird by the classroom door.

Finley always felt like Principal Small was watching her, and it made her nervous. It had started in kindergarten after the Play-Doh-in-the-toilet incident and had gotten worse last year after Principal Small had sampled Finley's super-spicy PB&J Pasta at the school cook-off.

Great, thought Finley. *She must have dropped in to see the convention. Clearly, this is not a good time to ask Ms. Bird for help.*

Chapter 12

GIVE BURPS A CHANCE

"It's your turn," Will said, pointing to Henry's desk.

"We mow dat!" Henry answered. He turned to Finley. "Cub od. Weff go!"

Finley and Henry made a beeline for their desks.

Olivia met them halfway across the room. "What is wrong with you guys?" she whispered. "Hurry up!"

"Mouff tuck," Henry said. Then he pointed toward his invention. "Oo elp?"

"What?" said Olivia. "Quit joking around — it's your turn!"

Henry shook his head. "Uh-uh. Mouff tuck. Bat tandy. Elp?"

Olivia shrugged. "I don't know what you're talking about!"

Finley grabbed a pencil from the desk beside her. She jotted down a note in her sketchbook and handed it to Olivia.

"Mouth stuck," Olivia read. "Bad candy. Help?"

Finley pointed to Henry's invention.

Olivia turned to Henry. "Are you kidding? You want *me* to demonstrate The Burpolator?"

Henry nodded, looking pitiful. "I oh oo bid," he said with his best lost-puppy eyes. Then he held out his notecards.

Finley grabbed her sketchbook back from Olivia and wrote: *He'll owe you big.*

Olivia read the note and rolled her eyes. Then she smoothed out her dress, straightened her hair bow, took Henry's notecards, and marched over to his desk just as the experts were starting to move on.

"Welcome!" Olivia said to the visitors. "Remember me — Olivia Snotham, the inventor of the marvelous Miss Manners? Well, I'm also Henry Lin's assistant. He's kind of speechless at the moment, so I'll be helping demonstrate his invention."

Olivia leafed through Henry's notecards, then shoved them into the pocket of her dress. She took a deep breath, cleared her throat, and held her head high. "Have you ever wanted to be a brilliant burper?" she began. "Have you ever wondered what it would be like to produce loud, satisfying, powerful belches?"

Henry looked at Finley, his eyes wide.

The experts exchanged worried glances. "Not really," said Mr. Wingnutt.

"Well," Olivia continued, unfazed, "The Burpolator can help you do just that." She patted Henry's invention — a giant cooler with plastic tubes coming out of it. "According to doctors, holding in burps can result in uncomfortable bloating, also known as tummy troubles. With The Burpolator, you can let it all out. So," she gave the experts her best mysterious look, "who's going first?"

Mr. Wingnutt and Dr. Clunk stepped back.

"Great," Olivia said, passing Mr. Quackenbottom one of the tubes that was dangling from the cooler. "It looks like you're the lucky one. The first step is . . ." She paused to read the instruction booklet on Henry's desk. "Take a long, refreshing, bubbly drink. Don't be shy — the bigger the drink, the more effective The Burpolator will be."

Mr. Quackenbottom examined the tube. "Is that really necessary?" he asked.

"I'm afraid so," said Olivia. "Look — it's so easy, even a kid can do it." She grabbed one of the plastic tubes and took a long drink. "Mmm. See? Now it's your turn."

Mr. Quackenbottom put the tube to his mouth, and took a tiny sip.

Olivia looked at Henry, who shook his head.

"It's going to take more than that," Olivia told Mr. Quackenbottom. "Pretend you're in the middle of the Sahara Desert. You're parched like a sad, dried-up little raisin. This is your first drink in days."

Mr. Quackenbottom hesitated, then guzzled down some of the liquid.

"Well done!" said Olivia. She checked the instruction booklet. "Next — jog in place for twenty seconds." She looked at her watch. "Ready . . . set . . . go!"

Olivia started jogging.

Mr. Quackenbottom just stood there, perplexed.

"If you don't do it, we'll have to start all over," Olivia warned.

Mr. Quackenbottom jogged in place.

"Okay, stop!" Olivia said twenty seconds later. "Time for the jumping jacks. Give me ten."

Mr. Quackenbottom glanced anxiously at Mr. Wingnutt and Dr. Clunk, then followed Olivia's directions.

"Now, relax and let it *aaalllll ooooout*," Olivia instructed.

Finley looked at Henry in amazement. Olivia was like one of those salespeople on TV.

Mr. Quackenbottom did not look relaxed.

"Close your eyes and visualize *biiiig* burps," Olivia coached.

Mr. Quackenbottom closed his eyes.

"Try opening your mouth just a bit," Olivia said.

Mr. Quackenbottom opened his mouth, but nothing came out.

"Huh," said Olivia. "I don't know why it's not working. The Burpolator has never failed before. Maybe someone else should try." She looked at Mr. Wingnutt.

Mr. Wingnutt glanced at Dr. Clunk. "Actually," he said briskly, "that's all the time we have for now."

Henry grabbed Finley's sketchbook and wrote: *Give burps a chance.* But the experts were already moving on to Finley's desk and were too busy writing their own notes to see.

Finley's stomach lurched. There was no way she could demonstrate the LaughCrafter with her mouth full of Reusable Space Candy. She had to act fast. She wasn't about to let some dumb gum prevent her from bringing joy to the world.

Chapter 13

A JOYFUL NOISE

Finley clawed at the roof of her mouth and scraped her nails against the back of her teeth. Then she hooked her finger around the Reusable Space Candy and yanked as hard as she could. It stretched as Finley struggled to keep a grip, but she kept pulling.

Suddenly, there was a sucking sound — followed by a loud *pop!* — as a big gob of gum flew out of Finley's mouth and landed right in the middle of Olivia's fake flower bouquet.

Finley took a deep breath. She was free. And just in time.

She tiptoed over to Olivia's desk and gently fished the Reusable Space Candy out of the flowers. Then she smushed it between two pages of her sketchbook and stuffed it into her pocket.

Mr. Wingnutt, Dr. Clunk, and Mr. Quackenbottom had just finished jotting down their notes when Finley slipped back to her desk. The experts gave a final nod to Olivia and Henry, then looked at Finley expectantly.

Finley stood behind the LaughCrafter. This was her big chance. She could almost hear the joyful noise of laughter ringing out around the world. She pictured a new Glendale Elementary School swimming pool and imagined Mom and Dad driving the family to get pizza in their new lime-green convertible.

Finley cleared her throat. "Hello," she said. "My name is Finley Flowers, and this is my invention —

the LaughCrafter. It's a known fact that laughing makes you healthier by reducing stress. Studies show that people live longer if they laugh a lot. Laughter truly is the best medicine. And the LaughCrafter is designed to help people laugh more. So step right up, and try it today!"

Mr. Wingnutt, Dr. Clunk, and Mr. Quackenbottom inched forward.

Finley handed them each a sheet of paper. "The LaughCrafter has several special attachments," she explained. "These easy instructions will tell you how to use them."

As the experts read the instructions, Finley stepped back beside Henry, who had grabbed the salad fork from Olivia's model table setting and was using it to pry the Reusable Space Candy out of his mouth.

Dr. Clunk put on the reading glasses that hung from a silver chain around her neck. She picked up the joke book.

Finley held her breath as the experts flipped through the pages of Henry's hilarious jokes. No one laughed. Not even a smile. "Uh-oh," she whispered. "They don't get the jokes."

"Maybe dere waffing on dee inhide," said Henry, picking the last bits of Reusable Space Candy out of his teeth.

"Laughing on the inside doesn't count," said Finley.

Dr. Clunk put the joke book down and picked up her instruction sheet.

Mr. Quackenbottom pressed the laugh-track button, and Evie's goofy giggling bubbled out of the speakers. Mr. Quackenbottom winced. Mr. Wingnutt looked puzzled. Dr. Clunk scribbled notes.

"The canned laughs aren't working either," whispered Henry.

"It's okay," Finley said. "The funny-face-maker is up next. Who can resist a funny face?"

The visitors read the instructions, then clustered around the funny-face-maker. They studied it with furrowed brows.

Maybe they need new glasses, Finley thought.

"You have to get close," she told Mr. Wingnutt, "so you can see."

Mr. Wingnutt got close. He peered into the upside-down mixing bowl. Then he smoothed his hair and straightened his tie.

Olivia wrote in her notebook and showed it to Finley. It read: *funny faces = fail*, with a frown-y face.

Finley sighed. "I've still got my secret weapon," she whispered. "Plan D: the toe-tickler."

"I dunno," said Henry. "They don't look ticklish."

"Sometimes those are the most ticklish ones," said Finley.

Dr. Clunk read her instruction sheet and examined the toe-tickler. She took off her shoe, held her foot up to the forest of feathers, and gave the wheel a spin. The feathers swept along her sole as the wheel slowed. When it stopped, Dr. Clunk straightened her sock matter-of-factly and put her shoe back on.

Drat, thought Finley.

Mr. Wingnutt went next. As the feathers touched his toes, Finley thought she saw his top lip quiver. But it must have been a nervous twitch. He finished his turn, then made room for Mr. Quackenbottom.

Double drat, thought Finley.

Mr. Quackenbottom bent down and put the attachment to his foot.

Come on, Finley thought. *Just a little giggle.*

She held her breath . . . but there was no joyful noise.

Suddenly Mr. Quackenbottom stood up, a strange expression taking over his face. His brow crinkled. His eyes bulged. He looked as if he might explode.

"BWAAAAH-HUH-WAAAAAAAAAH!" Mr. Quackenbottom burped the loudest, longest burp Finley had ever heard. It echoed across the room like a foghorn. Heads snapped to attention, and the whole class froze.

BWAAAH-HUH-WAAAH

Dr. Clunk's eyebrows shot up. Mr. Wingnutt jumped back. Mr. Quackenbottom put his hand to his mouth as if to stop anything else from escaping.

"Nice one, Mr. Quackenbottom!" said Henry. "I guess The Burpolator worked!"

"Excuse me," Mr. Quackenbottom muttered sheepishly.

"Looks like Miss Manners worked, too," Olivia said, beaming. "That was *very* polite."

But suddenly, Olivia's smile vanished. "UUUUUUUUUUUUUURP!" she belched, louder than a lawnmower. "Excuse *me*," she whispered. Then her face turned as red as her "NO BURPING" sign.

A smile tugged at the corners of Dr. Clunk's lips. Mr. Wingnutt let out a chuckle. Mr. Quackenbottom snorted. Then they all burst out laughing.

Finley, Henry, and Olivia couldn't help it. They started laughing, too.

"Yay!" Finley cheered. "I knew the LaughCrafter would work — it just needed a little help!"

Turning around, she saw Lia and Kate giggling. The laughter spark had finally caught, and now it was spreading like wildfire down the line of desks!

Soon the whole class was filled with tee-hee-ing, hooting, and howling. Will was doubled over holding his stomach, and Henry had started his crazy seal noises. Everyone was cracking up, and the more they laughed . . . the more they laughed.

As Finley glanced around, she pictured happy flames of laughter racing through the city and across the state. She imagined them flowing down rivers and flying on airplanes, spreading warmth and light across the country and the world!

"I think you need to put a warning label on the LaughCrafter," Henry said between gasps. "Use with caution — laughter is contagious!"

"Ow-ow-ow!" Olivia cried. "My stomach hurts!"
But she kept on laughing, wiping tears from her eyes.
Then suddenly, she stopped. "Uh-oh," she whispered
to Finley. "Here comes Principal Small."

Chapter 14

TEAM EFFORT

Finley spun around to see everyone looking in her direction. Principal Small was marching toward her, clip-clopping down the row of desks with Ms. Bird fluttering behind. She was a woman on a mission, and she was headed straight for Finley.

Finley's stomach lurched. She pictured Mom and Dad and Ms. Bird with their disappointed faces as Principal Small explained how Finley had disrupted the Invention Convention and was not a model fourth-grade citizen for Glendale Elementary School.

A lump grew in Finley's throat. *Maybe if I close my eyes and focus hard enough, I can sublimate myself,* she thought.

But when she opened them, Principal Small was standing right there. "Finley Flowers," she said like she was answering a question.

Finley smiled weakly. "Hello, Principal Small," she managed in her politest voice. "So nice to see you." She put out her hand and gave what she hoped was a firm-and-friendly handshake.

Principal Small pursed her lips together as she gestured to the LaughCrafter. "Is that what's responsible for this hullabaloo?"

Finley wasn't sure what hullabaloo was, but it didn't sound good. She glanced at Henry for help, but he was writing nervously in his notebook.

"Because it certainly livened up the Invention Convention," Principal Small continued. "I just wanted to see it for myself."

Finley breathed a sigh of relief. "Here it is," she said. "I call it the LaughCrafter. But it was really Henry's invention that made everyone laugh."

Henry grinned. "It was a team effort."

"Your inventions were both very creative," Ms. Bird chirped.

"Thanks," Finley and Henry said at once.

"What about mine?" Olivia piped up.

"Yours, too," said Ms. Bird. "Miss Manners saved the day." With that, she turned and walked Principal Small to the door.

"That reminds me," Olivia said to Henry. "You said you'd owe me for demonstrating The Burpolator. I think I did an excellent job."

"You did!" said Henry. "That was awesome!"

"So . . ." Olivia raised her eyebrows. "What do I get?"

Henry thought for a minute. "Unlimited lifetime use of The Burpolator. For *free!*"

Olivia shook her head. "No way. How about twenty bucks?"

"*Twenty bucks?*" Henry's eyebrows shot up.

Olivia shrugged. "That's a bargain. You said you'd owe me *big*, which means at least fifty, but I'll take twenty."

"Maybe you should wait," Finley suggested. "Someday you might need *his* help."

Olivia hesitated. "Fine," she said to Henry. "I guess it is kind of fun having you still owe me. Who knows when I might need something?"

Just then Ms. Bird rang the chime, and the class settled into silence. "It's time for our guests to go," she said, "but before they do, please join me in a round of applause to thank them for their time."

Everyone clapped. The special guests waved and smiled. Mr. Quackenbottom gave an awkward bow as they turned to go.

"I'll be passing out the feedback forms in a moment," Ms. Bird announced once the visitors had left, "but our guests wanted me to tell you they were very impressed."

Finley couldn't wait to read what the experts had to say about the LaughCrafter. They might have written a note offering to buy her idea! She held her breath as Ms. Bird darted around the room, calling out names: Will, Lia, Sam, Arpin, Kate . . .

"Finley Flowers!" Ms. Bird finally said, swooping in and sliding the feedback form onto Finley's desk.

Finley's heart pounded as she picked it up and read.

Henry leaned over in his seat. "So, what did they say?"

Finley finished reading, then set the paper down. "They said liked it," she said, frowning. "They really liked it."

Henry looked puzzled. "That's good, right? Why the sad face?"

"They *liked* it," Finley said. "But they didn't *love* it. And they didn't offer to buy my idea and sell it to the world."

Henry shrugged. "That doesn't mean you can't do it on your own."

Finley sighed. "I'm just a kid. I can't do anything on my own."

"Not true," said Henry. "You made the LaughCrafter. And look at Benjamin Franklin and all those other kid inventors. Besides, even if you had to wait till you were really old — like eighteen or even twenty — think of all of the other inventions you'd have by then!"

Finley groaned. "I'm not even ten yet. Twenty is a whole lifetime away!"

"Look, it just wasn't right for them," Henry said. "I mean, think about it — would you *really* want the LaughCrafter to be sold by the same company in charge of the collapsible toilet plunger or elephant-poo coffee filters?"

Finley tried to keep her frown down but couldn't. Henry always had a way of making her smile.

At recess, Finley and Henry headed for the swings. Finley pulled her sketchbook out of her pocket. "Ew," she said, peeking at the gummy goo that was sandwiched between the pages.

"I dunno about that Reusable Space Candy," Henry said with a shudder.

"I definitely won't be reusing it." Finley ripped out the sticky pages and threw them in the trash.

"But the LaughCrafter was great," Henry said, grabbing a swing.

"Thanks," said Finley, taking the next one over. "I can already think of one improvement, and the experts agreed."

"What?"

"A burp attachment," said Finley. "The Burpolator was definitely dazzling."

"Perfect!" said Henry. "The new and improved LaughCrafter Deluxe, now with built-in Burpolator! Or we could combine them — The BurpoLaughCrafter!"

"Sounds like a Hen-sational Fin-vention to me," said Finley. "I can't wait to try it out on Zack."

Finley leaned back and breathed in the cidery-sweet smell of fall. The wind whooshed through the branches above her, and a few orange and yellow leaves spiraled down. "Too bad I'm not going to make millions," she said. "I guess the LaughCrafter's not the next pet rock."

"Not yet," said Henry. "But bringing joy to the world is important. I think you should keep working on it. You make *me* laugh all the time."

Finley grinned. "You, too. A laugh machine is great. But nothing beats a Fin-tastic friend."

About the Author

Jessica Young grew up in Ontario, Canada. The same things make her happy now as when she was a kid: dancing, painting, music, digging in the dirt, picnics, reading, and writing. Like Finley Flowers, Jessica loves making stuff. When she was little, she wanted to be a tap-dancing flight attendant/veterinarian, but she's changed her mind! Jessica currently lives with her family in Nashville, Tennessee.

About the Illustrator

When Jessica Secheret was young, she had strange friends that were always with her: felt pens, colored pencils, brushes, and paint. After repainting all the walls in her house, her parents decided it was time for her to express her "talent" at an art school — the famous École Boulle in Paris. After several years at various architecture agencies, Jessica decided to give up squares, rulers, and compasses and dedicate her heart and soul to what she'd always loved — putting her own imagination on paper. Today, Jessica spends her time in her Paris studio, drawing for magazines and children's books in France and abroad.

What's New?
Invention Starter

What You'll Need:

- Sheet of white or lined paper
- Pencil or pen

What to Do:

Get inspired: Come up with a problem or something people need or want. As you go about your day, notice all of the helpful devices we use all the time. And think of all of the problems people need help with. Sometimes ideas can sprout when you least expect it — like when you're talking to friends or playing.

Write down your ideas: Be ready to remember your ideas! Carry a pencil and notebook around so you can jot them down. You can even make your own pocket-sized idea journal.

Research: Do some research to find out more. Does anything like your idea already exist? If so, how can you make that same idea even better?

Name it: Think of a great name for your idea, something that sounds fun or interesting and lets people know what it is.

Draw it: Make a drawing or diagram of your invention. Don't forget to label the parts!

Write it: Write a description of your invention. Describe how you got your idea and what your invention does.

Build it: Make sure to have an adult supervise or help. Explain your invention and get permission to use your building materials to make a 3-D model of your invention.

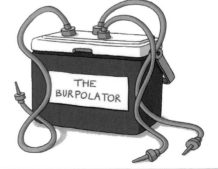